Peppa Pig ™

Peppa Goes Skiing

It is a lovely snowy day and Peppa's family are going skiing. First, they have to take a ski lift all the way to the top of Snowy Mountain. "Oh . . . that looks a bit high," says Daddy Pig. Daddy Pig does not like heights.

Everyone gets on the ski lift.
"This is fun!" calls Peppa, and
she sings a little song.

"In the air!
In a chair!
Snow is falling
everywhere!"

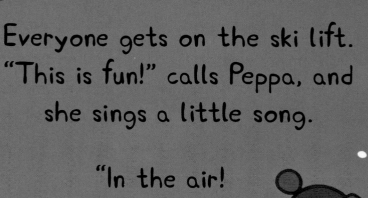

Hee
Hee
Hee

Clunk

Clank

Daddy Pig does not think it is fun.
He does not like the way
the ski lift clunks and clanks.

At the top of
Snowy Mountain,
Daddy Pig falls out
of his chair and
into the snow!

"Are you all right, Daddy?" cries Peppa.

"Ho ho! Yes, Peppa," says Daddy Pig. "Let's get you to your ski lesson."

Whoosh!

Madame Gazelle starts the
ski lesson. Peppa, George and
all their friends learn how
to start and stop.

"Weeee! Skiing is fun!"
cries Peppa, as they go
down the baby slope.

"Can we see you ski now,
Madame Gazelle?" asks Peppa.

"Oh, I don't know . . ." replies Madame Gazelle.
"Please!" everyone cries.
"Very well," says Madame Gazelle.

Voila! Madame Gazelle does a magnificent ski jump.

Everyone claps and cheers.

"That was amazing!" says Peppa.
"Thank you," says Madame Gazelle.
"I was the world champion at
skiing and I won this cup!"
"Ooooh," everyone says.

"Which mummy or daddy would like a go?" asks Madame Gazelle.
"I will!" says Mummy Pig.
"Where does this path lead?"
"Down the mountain!" cries Madame Gazelle.

"Help! Where are the brakes?" shouts Mummy Pig.

"She can't stop!" cries Daddy Pig.
"Let's catch up with her in the coach!"

Mummy Pig skis down the mountain,
along the road and past the shops!
"Eeeeeeeeee! Stand back!" cries Mummy Pig.
She even does a loop the loop at top speed!

Finally, everyone catches up with Mummy Pig.
She has crashed straight into a snowdrift!
"Snort! You're a walking, talking
snowman, Mummy!" laughs Peppa.

"I have never seen such amazing skiing," says
Madame Gazelle. "This cup belongs to you now!"

Everyone cheers, as Madame Gazelle presents
Mummy Pig with her world champion cup.
"Hooray!" says Peppa. "My mummy is a skiing champion!"